MISSOURI

Julie Murray

VISIT US AT
www.abdopublishing.com

Published by ABDO Publishing Company, PO Box 398166, Minneapolis, MN 55439.

Copyright © 2013 by Abdo Consulting Group, Inc. International copyrights reserved in all countries. No part of this book may be reproduced in any form without written permission from the publisher. Big Buddy Books™ is a trademark and logo of ABDO Publishing Company.

Printed in the United States of America, North Mankato, Minnesota.
042012
092012

 PRINTED ON RECYCLED PAPER

Coordinating Series Editor: Rochelle Baltzer
Editor: Sarah Tieck
Contributing Editors: Megan M. Gunderson, BreAnn Rumsch, Marcia Zappa
Graphic Design: Adam Craven
Cover Photograph: *iStockphoto*: ©iStockphoto.com/Veni.
Interior Photographs/Illustrations: *Alamy*: PhotoStock-Israel (p. 11); *AP Photo*: AP Photo (pp. 13, 23, 25), James A. Finley (p. 27), Tom Gannam (p. 21), North Wind Picture Archives via AP Images (p. 13), Jeff Roberson (p. 19); *Getty Images*: Kevin Hovan (p. 5), Jamie Squire (p. 21); *Glow Images*: Imagebroker RM (p. 26); *iStockphoto*: ©iStockphoto.com/ramonailumuscom (p. 26), ©iStockphoto.com/RiverNorthPhotography (p. 19), ©iStockphoto.com/tjmacphoto (p. 17), ©iStockphoto.com/tomorrowspix (p. 9); *Shutterstock*: Nina B (p. 27), Sharon Day (p. 29), Ffooter (p. 27), Karen Kaspar (p. 30), Philip Lange (p. 30), Brian Lasenby (p. 30), Henryk Sadura (p. 9), Steven Russell Smith Photos/Shutterstock (p. 30).

All population figures taken from the 2010 US census.

Library of Congress Cataloging-in-Publication Data

Murray, Julie, 1969-
  Missouri / Julie Murray.
     p. cm. -- (Explore the United States)
  ISBN 978-1-61783-363-2
  1. Missouri--Juvenile literature. I. Title.
  F466.3.M873 2013
  977.8--dc23
                    2012007063

Contents

ONE NATION

The United States is a **diverse** country. It has farmland, cities, coasts, and mountains. Its people come from many different backgrounds. And, its history covers more than 200 years.

Today the country includes 50 states. Missouri is one of these states. Let's learn more about this state and its story!

Did You Know?

Missouri became a state on August 10, 1821. It was the twenty-fourth state to join the nation.

The Mississippi (*above*) and the
Missouri Rivers meet in Missouri.

MISSOURI UP CLOSE

The United States has four main **regions**. Missouri is in the Midwest.

Missouri has eight states on its borders. Iowa is north. Nebraska, Kansas, and Oklahoma are west. Arkansas is south. Illinois, Kentucky, and Tennessee are east.

Missouri has a total area of 69,703 square miles (180,530 sq km). About 6 million people live there.

REGIONS OF THE UNITED STATES

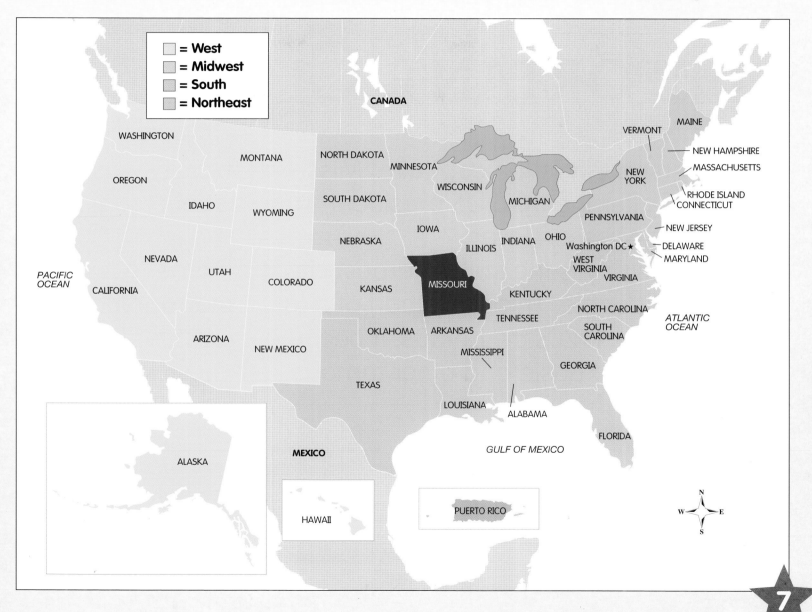

= West
= Midwest
= South
= Northeast

CANADA

WASHINGTON
MONTANA
NORTH DAKOTA
MINNESOTA
OREGON
IDAHO
WYOMING
SOUTH DAKOTA
WISCONSIN
MICHIGAN
VERMONT
MAINE
NEW HAMPSHIRE
MASSACHUSETTS
NEW YORK
RHODE ISLAND
CONNECTICUT
IOWA
NEBRASKA
ILLINOIS
INDIANA
OHIO
PENNSYLVANIA
NEW JERSEY
NEVADA
UTAH
COLORADO
KANSAS
MISSOURI
Washington DC★
DELAWARE
MARYLAND
WEST VIRGINIA
VIRGINIA
PACIFIC OCEAN
CALIFORNIA
KENTUCKY
NORTH CAROLINA
ATLANTIC OCEAN
TENNESSEE
SOUTH CAROLINA
ARIZONA
NEW MEXICO
OKLAHOMA
ARKANSAS
MISSISSIPPI
GEORGIA
TEXAS
LOUISIANA
ALABAMA
FLORIDA
GULF OF MEXICO
ALASKA
MEXICO
HAWAII
PUERTO RICO

N
W   E
S

7

IMPORTANT CITIES

Jefferson City is the **capital** of Missouri. This city was named after the third US president, Thomas Jefferson. It is on the Missouri River.

Kansas City is the state's largest city. It is home to 459,787 people. This city is part of a large **metropolitan** area. In the 1920s and 1930s, it became known for jazz music. Count Basie and other famous jazz musicians started out there.

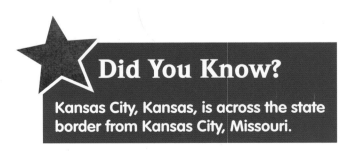

Did You Know?

Kansas City, Kansas, is across the state border from Kansas City, Missouri.

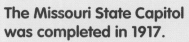
The Missouri State Capitol
was completed in 1917.

Missouri

Kansas City

Saint Louis

Jefferson City

Springfield

Kansas City is on the Missouri River.

9

Saint Louis is Missouri's second-largest city. Its population is 319,294. In 1764, Saint Louis became one of the first settlements in present-day Missouri. It is home to the tallest US monument, the Gateway Arch.

Springfield is the state's third-largest city, with 159,498 people. Many people stay in the city to visit the nearby Ozark Mountains.

Forest Park is a city park in Saint Louis. It is home to the Saint Louis Zoo and other popular spots.

MISSOURI IN HISTORY

The history of Missouri includes Native Americans, explorers, and the **Louisiana Purchase**. Native Americans have lived in the area for thousands of years. Around 1673, the French began exploring the land. Over time, they settled it.

In 1803, the United States bought a large piece of land from France. This was called the Louisiana Purchase. The land included present-day Missouri. Missouri became a US territory in 1812 and a state in 1821.

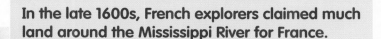
In the late 1600s, French explorers claimed much land around the Mississippi River for France.

President Thomas Jefferson arranged for the Louisiana Purchase. This almost doubled the size of the United States!

13

Timeline

1804

Meriwether Lewis and William Clark began exploring what is now the western United States. They started their journey near Saint Louis.

1821

Missouri became the twenty-fourth state on August 10.

1904

The **Louisiana Purchase** Exposition was held in Saint Louis. It honored the 100th anniversary of the purchase. The first ice cream cone was served there!

1800s

1811

The first of three large earthquakes hit Missouri. They were some of the strongest ever recorded in the United States.

1860

Pony Express riders began delivering mail on horseback. They traveled between Missouri and California.

1873

The nation's first public kindergarten opened in Saint Louis.

14

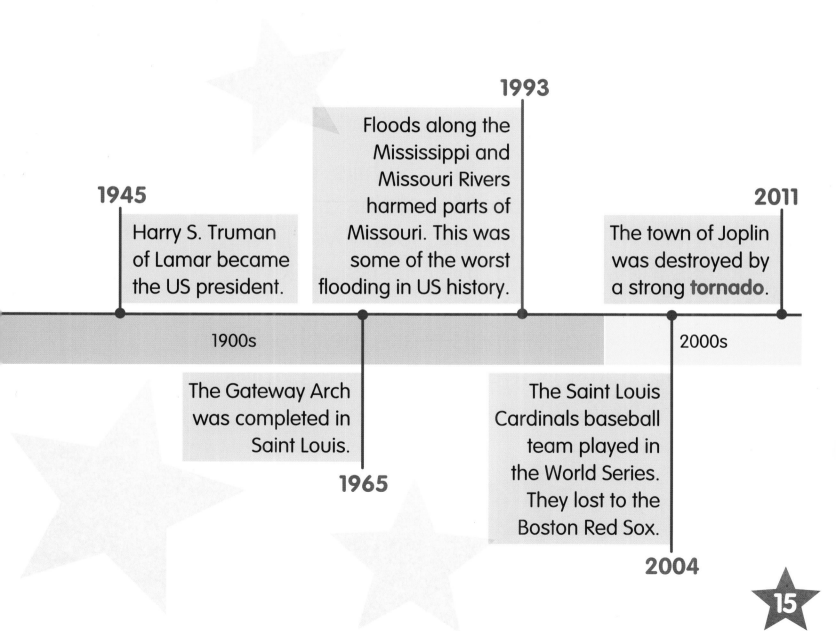

1993

Floods along the Mississippi and Missouri Rivers harmed parts of Missouri. This was some of the worst flooding in US history.

1945

Harry S. Truman of Lamar became the US president.

2011

The town of Joplin was destroyed by a strong **tornado**.

1900s

2000s

The Gateway Arch was completed in Saint Louis.

1965

The Saint Louis Cardinals baseball team played in the World Series. They lost to the Boston Red Sox.

2004

ACROSS THE LAND

Missouri has **plains**, forests, hills, and mountains. The Ozark Mountains are in southern Missouri. The Missouri River flows across the state. And, the Mississippi River forms its eastern border.

Many types of animals make their homes in Missouri. Some of these include white-tailed deer, beavers, and woodpeckers.

Did You Know?

In July, the average temperature in Missouri is 78°F (26°C). In January, it is 30°F (-1°C).

Forests cover much of the Ozark Mountains.
Lakes, springs, and streams are also common.

17

Earning a Living

Missouri has many different areas of business. Finance, health care, and manufacturing are important. Farmers raise livestock and grow crops such as soybeans and hay. And, many people have jobs with the government or helping visitors.

Journalism has strong ties in Missouri. In 1878, Joseph Pulitzer created the *Saint Louis Post-Dispatch*. It is still a major newspaper today. In 1908, the University of Missouri at Columbia opened the world's first journalism school.

Did You Know?

Pulitzer Prizes are important arts awards. They were started by Joseph Pulitzer. Several are given each year for excellence in journalism.

The state's manufacturing companies make food products, aircraft, and automobiles (*right*).

Kansas City is home to Hallmark Cards. This is one of the biggest US card makers.

19

Sports Page

Missouri is home to many sports teams. The state's football teams are the Saint Louis Rams and the Kansas City Chiefs. Its baseball teams are the Kansas City Royals and the Saint Louis Cardinals. Missouri's hockey team is the Saint Louis Blues.

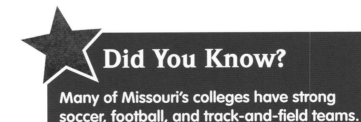

Did You Know?

Many of Missouri's colleges have strong soccer, football, and track-and-field teams.

Missouri fans are often excited to support their favorite teams!

HOMETOWN HEROES

Many famous people are from Missouri. Harry S. Truman was born in Lamar in 1884. He was the US president from 1945 to 1953.

Truman became vice president in January 1945. In April, he became president after Franklin D. Roosevelt died. At this time, the United States was fighting in **World War II**. Truman helped end the war.

Truman was the thirty-third US president.

Mark Twain was born in the small town of Florida in 1835. He was a famous author.

Twain wrote many well-known books. These include *The Adventures of Tom Sawyer* and *Adventures of Huckleberry Finn*. These stories are about life on and around the Mississippi River.

Mark Twain's real name was Samuel Clemens.

Tour Book

Do you want to go to Missouri? If you visit the state, here are some places to go and things to do!

 **Taste**

Try some Kansas City barbecue. This area has a special way of cooking barbecue. Meat is smoked over wood and covered in a tomato and molasses sauce.

 Explore

Missouri has more than 6,000 caves! Visit the Meramec Caverns in Stanton. Some say famous outlaws like Jesse James hid from lawmen in them!

 Hike

Visit Mark Twain National Forest in the Ozark Mountains. People hike, bike, and camp there.

Discover

The Gateway Arch is 630 feet (192 m) tall! Take a tram ride to the top for a great view. You can see the city of Saint Louis (*right*) and western Illinois.

 Cheer

Catch a baseball game at Busch Stadium in Saint Louis. Fans that arrive early may be able to see the Cardinals practice!

A GREAT STATE

The story of Missouri is important to the United States. The people and places that make up this state offer something special to the country. Together with all the states, Missouri helps make the United States great.

Kansas City's many fountains earned it the nickname "the City of Fountains."

Fast Facts

Date of Statehood:
August 10, 1821

Population (rank):
5,988,927
(18th most-populated state)

Total Area (rank):
69,703 square miles
(20th largest state)

Motto:
"Salus Populi Suprema
Lex Esto"
(The Welfare of the People
Shall Be the Supreme Law)

Nickname:
Show Me State

State Capital:
Jefferson City

Flag:

Flower: Hawthorn Blossom

Postal Abbreviation:
MO

Tree: Flowering Dogwood

Bird: Eastern Bluebird

Important Words

capital a city where government leaders meet.

diverse made up of things that are different from each other.

journalism the practice of reporting, writing, and editing news.

Louisiana Purchase land the United States purchased from France in 1803. It extended from the Mississippi River to the Rocky Mountains and from Canada through the Gulf of Mexico.

metropolitan of or relating to a large city, usually with nearby smaller cities called suburbs.

plains flat or rolling land without trees.

region a large part of a country that is different from other parts.

tornado a strong wind with a funnel-shaped cloud. A tornado moves in a narrow path.

World War II a war fought in Europe, Asia, and Africa from 1939 to 1945.

Web Sites

To learn more about Missouri, visit ABDO Publishing Company online. Web sites about Missouri are featured on our Book Links page. These links are routinely monitored and updated to provide the most current information available.

www.abdopublishing.com

Index